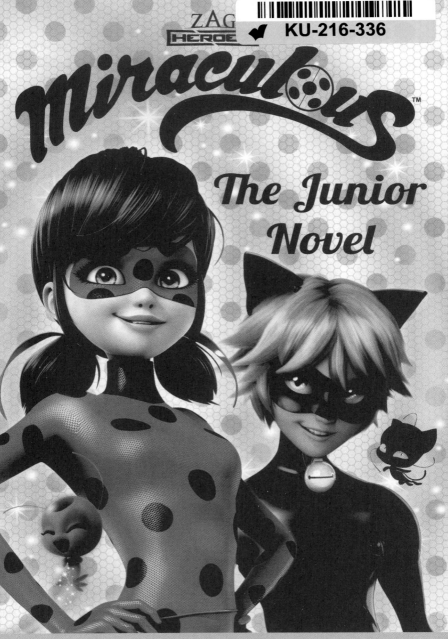

ZAG
HEROES

Miraculous™

The Junior Novel

igloobooks

iglooabooks

Published in 2017
by Igloo Books Ltd
Cottage Farm
Sywell
NN6 0BJ
www.igloobooks.com

Cover designed by Tim Robins
Written by Gemma Barder
Edited by Gemma Rose

LEO002 0917
2 4 6 8 10 9 7 5 3 1
ISBN 978-1-78670-964-6

Printed and manufactured in China

CONTENTS

PROLOGUE

The Miraculous

Many centuries ago, jewels bestowed with extraordinary powers were created.

These jewels were called the Miraculous.

Throughout history, the jewels were used for the good of the human race. To fight battles, defeat hideous creatures and keep the world safe from those who would seek to rule for the force of evil.

Each jewel was unique and precious, holding within it its own special powers and abilities:

a golden bee comb, a turtle bracelet, a peacock brooch, a fox-tail necklace, a moth brooch and, most powerful of all, a pair of ladybug earrings and a cat's paw ring.

The ladybug earrings granted the wearer the power of creation, the ability to create the perfect object to help the wearer battle against evil. This ability was called Lucky Charm. The cat's paw ring, in balance, gave the power of destruction. Once summoned, the power of Cataclysm could destroy in one touch.

According to legend, whoever held these two Miraculouses at the same time would achieve absolute power.

A tall, thin man stood in an empty room. Shafts of sunlight fell on him as he stroked a picture of a young woman inside a small purple brooch. In the light, hundreds of glowing moths fluttered lazily here and there and rested by the man's feet. "I WANT that absolute power, Nooroo," the man said, snapping the brooch shut. "The ladybug earrings and the cat's paw ring must be mine!"

Nooroo was a small, sprite-like creature called a kwami who shimmered with a lilac glow. He belonged to the moth brooch Miraculous and his purpose in life was to help whoever possessed the brooch to use its formidable powers. "But no one knows where these Miraculouses are," Nooroo said, pleadingly.

The tall man smiled nastily. "I found you though, my little Nooroo," he sneered. "It shouldn't be too difficult for me to find the others. Tell me again what my Miraculous does, Nooroo."

Despite the dark feeling he felt in his stomach, Nooroo felt a little brighter. Talking about his Miraculous was one of his favourite things to do.

"The moth brooch allows you to give someone their own superpowers. In turn, that person will become your devoted follower."

The thin man clasped his hands around the brooch. A vicious smile spread across his face giving Nooroo a growing sense of dread. "Then there is only one clear path in front of me. Those who possess the ladybug earrings and the cat's paw ring will become formidable superheroes, and what could be better for luring superheroes than to create my very own supervillain? Once these superheroes appear, and defend the innocent people of Paris, that is when I shall capture their Miraculouses!"

Nooroo gulped. "Master, the Miraculous are not meant to be used for evil purposes," he implored.

The thin man stomped his foot sending a cloud of moths fluttering around him. "I MUST HAVE THIS ABSOLUTE POWER!" he roared. "Your Miraculous is in MY control. I am your master now and you must OBEY ME!"

Nooroo bowed his head. As much as he wished it wasn't so, ancient magic forced him to do whatever the thin man wanted. "Yes, Master," he sighed, unhappily.

The thin man attached the brooch to his lapel and called, "Dark wings, rise!" Suddenly, some of the fluttering moths clung to the thin man creating a suit of deep purple and a shining silver mask. Nooroo whimpered as he, too, became part of the thin man's armour.

"From this day on I shall be known as Hawk Moth!" Hawk Moth started laughing. "The Miraculous will be mine and nothing can stop me!"

Across Paris, another little kwami called Wayzz was taking a nap when he felt something

wake him with a start. "Master! Master!" Wayzz called. "I have felt the moth Miraculous' aura!"

Wayzz's master was a kind, elderly man called Master Fu. "I thought it had been lost forever," he mused, stroking his beard.

"But Master, it was a negative aura. I fear it might have fallen into the hands of a negative power."

Master Fu nodded. "We must find Nooroo and his Miraculous. If it has gotten into the wrong hands, who knows what evil it could bring on the world." Master Fu raised his arm to reveal the turtle bracelet Miraculous. "Time to transform!" he called. But instead of turning into a superhero, Master Fu stumbled.

Wayzz flew to his master's side. "Please Master, be reasonable, you are—"

"Still young!" protested Master Fu. "But you are right, Wayzz. I can no longer do this alone. I'm going to need some help."

Master Fu approached an old gramophone and punched a secret code into the side to reveal a jewellery box containing the secret missing Miraculouses.

CHAPTER ONE

Back To School

Marinette snuggled deeper under her duvet, ignoring the persistent buzzing of her phone's alarm. If she just stayed inside her cosy sheets a little longer maybe, just maybe, she could pretend today wasn't happening.

"Marinette! Your alarm's been going off for fifteen minutes!" Marinette's mother called from the kitchen. "You're going to be late for your first day back at school!"

It was no use. Sooner or later Marinette was

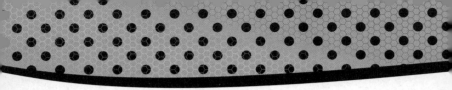

going to have to give in. Lazily, she grabbed her phone and killed the alarm. "Coming, Mum," she sighed.

Sabine Dupain-Cheng smiled as her daughter sleepily flopped down the stairs to the kitchen. Marinette was already taller than her mother and growing up fast. She let out a big sigh as she hopped onto a stool and poured her cereal.

"I bet Chloé will be in my class again," Marinette said, hopelessly. Chloé was the girl who had made Marinette's life miserable for four years in a row. She was rich, blonde, perfect in every way apart from the fact that, for some unknown reason, she hated Marinette. "Lucky me."

"Don't say that!" Sabine said, cheerfully. "It's the start of a new year. I'm sure everything will be just fine."

Marinette smiled. Somehow her mum always

knew just the right thing to say to make her feel better. Maybe it would be okay. Maybe she would stroll into school without tripping over or bumping into Chloé. Maybe she would ace all her classes and be the most popular girl in school, and maybe she would get accepted onto the coolest fashion course in Paris. As she turned back to her breakfast, Marinette knocked the fruit bowl with her elbow and sent a satsuma flying into the air while simultaneously knocking over the milk carton. Then again, maybe not.

When Marinette had changed into her favourite pink jeans, embroidered T-shirt and black jacket, she started to feel a little better. Tom, Marinette's dad, had been working in the family bakery since the early hours. As Marinette bounded in she was greeted with the familiar smell of fresh bread and sweet patisserie.

Marinette loved seeing her dad, who was possibly the tallest, largest baker in Paris, create

rows upon rows of dainty confectionery, especially when he made them just for her.

"Dad! These are so awesome!" Marinette squealed as her dad handed her a box of lime-flavoured macaroons.

"Glad you like them," Tom grinned.

Marinette closed the box carefully. "My class will love them!" *And they might just keep Chloé off my back,* she thought. "You're the best."

Tom reached behind him and grabbed a black sketchbook. "No, we're the best," he said, flipping to a sketch of the bakery's new logo. "Thanks to your amazing designs."

Marinette beamed with pride. Her dad always believed in her and supported her scribbling. She threw her arms around his neck, sending the box of macaroons into the air. Luckily, both Sabine and Tom were used to their daughter's clumsiness and had become skilled at catching anything Marinette sent flying.

"See you tonight!" Marinette called, dashing out of the bakery before she could knock over anything else.

It was a beautiful day as Marinette stepped out onto the busy streets of Paris. As she looked up and down the road, Marinette noticed an elderly man with a walking stick struggling to cross the street. Suddenly, a car rounded the corner at speed and sounded its horn, urging the elderly man to move faster. Marinette was horrified. If the elderly man didn't pick up pace he was going to get run over!

No one else seemed to notice what was about to happen. Marinette had to do something. She mustered all her courage and dashed into the road, gently taking the elderly man's elbow and quickly guiding him to the pavement. Unfortunately, Marinette also tripped on the kerb, sending her box of lime-flavoured treats crashing to the floor.

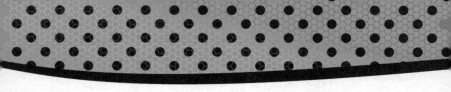

"Thank you, Miss," said the elderly man. He looked at the broken macaroons and shook his head disappointedly. "Oh, dear. What a disaster," he sighed.

Marinette stood up and rescued the box from under the feet of busy Parisians on their way to work. "Don't worry, I'm no stranger to disaster," she smiled. "Besides, there are a few left."

"May I?" asked the elderly man, delving into the box to sample one for himself. "Delicious!" he declared.

Just then, the air filled with the sound of a ringing school bell and Marinette suddenly remembered the reason she was up so early carrying a box of macaroons in the first place. "Oh, no! I'm going to be late." Marinette made a polite bow. "Have a nice day, sir!" Then she dashed off towards her school, leaving the elderly man watching her with a knowing smile.

glasses and Marinette smiled. No one glared at Chloé. This new girl had guts.

"Listen," ordered Chloé, turning back to Marinette. "Adrien is starting school today and he will want his closest friend to sit behind him. That's not you. That's me. So move, okay?"

Marinette stared at the empty desk in front of her. "Who's Adrien?" she asked.

Chloé and Sabrina screamed with laughter. "Can you believe she doesn't know who Adrien is?" Chloé said to Sabrina, as though Marinette no longer existed. "What rock has she been living under?"

"He's only a famous model!" Sabrina said, dreamily.

"And he's MY best friend," declared Chloé. "He ADORES me, so MOVE!"

Marinette was just about to give in when the new girl appeared behind Chloé. Startled, Chloé spun round. "Who elected you Queen of

Seats?" asked the new girl, folding her arms and staring straight at Chloé.

"Oh, look, Sabrina!" Chloé trilled in a sing-song voice. "We've got a do-gooder in our class. What are you going to do? Shoot laser beams out of your glasses?"

The new girl didn't budge. She'd seen girls like Chloé before and they didn't frighten her in the slightest. "Wouldn't you like to know?"

With that, the new girl grabbed Marinette and pulled her into the seat next to her. "Come on," she said, as Marinette tripped on her way, sending all but one of her remaining macaroons smashing to the classroom floor.

"Sorry, sorry, sorry!" Marinette said, scooping up the box.

"Chillax, girl!" said the new girl, smiling. "It's no biggie."

Marinette sighed. The new girl seemed so confident. "I wish I could handle Chloé the way you do," she said.

The new girl pulled out her phone and showed Marinette a picture of a superhero in flight. "You mean the way Majestia does," she beamed. Marinette looked confused. "Majestia says: 'All that is necessary for the triumph of evil is for good people to do nothing.'" She put her hand on Marinette's shoulder and pointed at Chloé. "That girl over there is evil and we're the good people!"

Marinette loved the idea of standing up to Chloé, but it seemed impossible. "She makes my life miserable," Marinette sighed.

The new girl shook her head. "That's because you let her. You need more confidence!"

Just being around this girl gave Marinette a boost. She fished out the last-surviving macaroon from the bakery box, broke it in half and gave a piece to her new friend. "I'm Marinette," she said, introducing herself.

The new girl grinned as she took the treat. "I'm Alya," she replied.

Maybe this year wasn't going to be so bad after all.

CHAPTER THREE

The Note

*A*drien Agreste was not like other boys. Sure, he was a world-famous model, lived in a mansion in absolute luxury and his father was an internationally recognised fashion designer, but that wasn't what set him apart. The real reason that Adrien was so different to nearly every other boy his age in Paris was that Adrien really, really, really wanted to go to school.

The only thing stopping Adrien achieving his goal was his father. Gabriel Agreste had kept

Adrien at home to be schooled by his assistant, Nathalie Sancoeur, ever since Adrien's mother had gone missing years ago. Unable to free himself from his dad's protective grip, Adrien had become resentful of his dad and was desperate to experience a normal life.

Today was going to be different. Today, Adrien had decided that another school year was not going to start without him being present, even if that meant running the whole way there while trying to avoid his bodyguard and Nathalie.

Adrien had just reached the front steps of Collège Françoise Dupont when the screeching tyres of an expensive black car made him stop.

"Adrien, please reconsider," Nathalie cried as she leapt from the back of the car. "You know what your father wants."

Adrien was furious. Furious at Nathalie for following him and furious at himself that he hadn't been able to outrun her. "But this is what I want to do," he said angrily, turning to climb the steps of the school.

Then something made Adrien stop.

An elderly man had stumbled on the pavement nearby and was struggling to reach his walking stick. Adrien forgot all about school and dashed to help, handing the walking stick back and helping the elderly man to his feet.

"Thank you, young man," the elderly man said, a wide smile covering his small face. Adrien smiled back, feeling happy he could help.

But Adrien's elation vanished as soon as he turned back to the school. Nathalie wasn't going to let him get past her. Slowly, Adrien gave in and slumped back to his captors. "I just want to be like everyone else," he sighed. "Please don't tell my father about this."

As Adrien let himself be led back to the black car, the elderly man stood up straight and watched, whistling to himself. Master Fu had

found another good soul to help him with his plan.

Inside school, the bell rang to signal the end of the morning lessons. Chloé was devastated that Adrien hadn't shown up. She groaned as she grabbed her bag and sloped out of the classroom with Sabrina in tow.

Behind Chloé, a smug, self-satisfied boy named Kim passed a note across his table to one of his classmates, Ivan, who was easily a foot taller than Kim and about three times as broad.

As he read Kim's note, Ivan's face flushed and his eyes narrowed. Anger flared up inside Ivan as he balled the note up in his hand and aimed his fist at Kim's face. "Kim!" he roared, but before he had a chance to land a blow on Kim's now rather frightened face, Miss Bustier stepped in.

"Ivan! Go to the Principal's office!" she demanded.

Ivan dropped his fist. He knew that if he explained what was in Kim's note to Miss Bustier, she might understand why he was so angry, but Ivan was too embarrassed to say anything. Instead, he clenched the note tighter in his hand and stomped out of the classroom, leaving Kim smiling smugly behind him.

In a secret lair, not far from the school, Hawk Moth and his winged creatures were alerted. "Negative emotions..." Hawk Moth said, smiling, breathing them in. "This is perfect. Just what I need for my plan to work. I can feel the anger and sadness this boy possesses."

Hawk Moth held out his hand and a moth landed gently on his palm. "Burn a hole in his heart, my horrible akuma." Hawk Moth closed

his hands around the moth, filling it with evil and turning it as black as night. "Fly away, my little akuma, and evilise him."

The akuma fluttered out of the large window of the lair towards Marinette's school. It knew the job it had to do, and the boy who was its target.

Meanwhile, Ivan had arrived at the Principal's office. He was still furious about the note that Kim had written and couldn't let go of it. He burst into the Principal's office.

"Excuse me, young man," said the Principal, looking up from his papers. "Didn't anyone ever teach you to knock?"

Ivan huffed back out into the hall, feeling his anger and frustration growing like a ball of fire inside him. At that same moment, Hawk Moth's akuma landed on Ivan's balled-up note, sending a shock wave through his body. Suddenly, Ivan was able to hear Hawk Moth's voice inside his head. The akuma had done its job: Ivan's mind and body were now under Hawk Moth's control.

"Stoneheart," Hawk Moth began, giving Ivan his new supervillain name. "I am Hawk Moth. I grant you the power to seek revenge on those who have wronged you."

Ivan was no longer Ivan. He was becoming Stoneheart. His body changed from that of a teenage boy to a giant, stone creature full of hatred and revenge. He no longer had to knock at the Principal's door, he could knock it down instead. "KIM!" Stoneheart roared as the Principal screamed and hid under the desk.

Stoneheart's roar was so loud it shook the school to its core, knocking Marinette and Alya off their seats as they chatted in the library.

Students were screaming and running in every direction. Marinette felt herself being

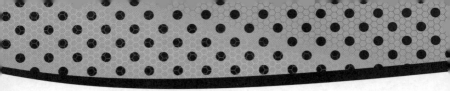

pulled to her feet as Alya dragged her to the library's CCTV cameras. Marinette watched as Stoneheart leapt out of the Principal's window, screaming Kim's name.

"What's going on?" Marinette asked, confused and frightened. "He has Ivan's voice?!"

Alya, on the other hand, was anything but frightened. She jumped up and down with glee. "It's as if he's been transformed into a REAL-LIFE supervillain!" she squealed, as she rummaged through her bag. "GPS? Check. Battery? Check. Where there's a supervillain there's always a superhero close behind!"

Alya ran outside, desperate to spot a real-life superhero at last, leaving Marinette to stare at the CCTV screens in horror. Marinette decided to run to the safest place she could think of.

Home.

CHAPTER FOUR

Small Black Boxes

Outside the imposing gates of a palatial mansion, Master Fu waited. He had a job to do, and it was only a matter of waiting for the right moment to get it done.

Inside, Adrien was sitting at a long dining table learning French history from Nathalie. Adrien was smart, very smart. He sighed as he reeled off fact after fact, dodging any trick questions Nathalie threw in to try and trip him up.

When Gabriel Agreste entered a room, everyone took notice – except for Adrien, who was the one person in Paris who wasn't impressed by his dad. Gabriel was tall and thin, and everything about him was neat and precise. From his hair right down to his perfectly polished shoes, nothing was out of place. Nathalie lowered her clipboard obediently as Adrien rolled his eyes.

"Give me a minute, please, Nathalie," Gabriel said in an authoritative voice, then he turned his attention to Adrien. "You are NOT going to school! We've been through this."

Adrien shot a look at Nathalie. Despite asking her not to, she had betrayed him and told his father what he had done that morning.

"Everything you need is right here," Gabriel continued. "I will NOT have you going outside into that dangerous world."

"It's not dangerous, father," Adrien protested.

"I'm always stuck in here by myself. Why can't I make friends just like everybody else?"

"BECAUSE YOU ARE NOT LIKE EVERYBODY ELSE. YOU ARE MY SON!" Gabriel boomed. "Continue with the teaching, Nathalie."

Adrien's father left the room and Nathalie tried to sound upbeat as she told Adrien they didn't have to carry on lessons if he didn't want to. But Adrien didn't want to listen. He ran past the portrait of his mother and father, back when their family was complete, and slammed his bedroom door shut.

Outside Adrien's house, another conflict was raging. The police had managed to surround Stoneheart as he stomped his way through Paris. They opened fire, but instead of wounding the creature, Stoneheart grew in size with each shot that hit him.

Buoyed by his new strength, Stoneheart

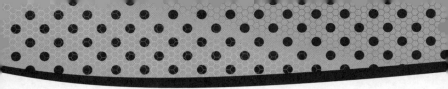

picked up a police van and hurled it through the air.

Hearing the commotion, Adrien switched on the plasma TV in his room and watched in amazement as the news showed him images of a real-life supervillain attacking just metres away from his bedroom window. Adrien was so absorbed in the news that, at first, he didn't spot the small black box that had appeared on his coffee table.

"What's this doing here?"

"What's this doing here?"

Marinette was also in her room, but she was there out of choice. Stoneheart had her terrified and she was hiding behind her desk chair, as if it could have protected her from a twenty-foot tall supervillain made of stone.

Her eyes had slipped from the screen, just

for a moment, to her desk where a small, black box had appeared. Marinette slowly opened it up to reveal a beautiful pair of red, spotted earrings. She barely had a chance to look at them before a ball of light filled the air, popping to reveal a floating little red kwami.

Marinette screamed and backed away as fast as she could. Unlike Master Fu, she had never seen a kwami before and, to her, this floating creature could have been anything from an over-sized bug to a miniature ghost.

"Everything's okay," said the kwami in a sweet voice. "Don't be scared." Marinette started throwing anything she could lay her hands on at the kwami. "Listen, Marinette," the kwami continued, easily swooping out of the way of each missile Marinette threw her way. "I know this might seem a bit strange to you—"

Suddenly Marinette grabbed a glass and trapped the kwami inside.

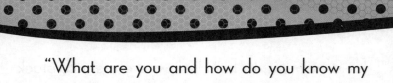

"What are you and how do you know my name?" Marinette demanded.

The kwami smiled. "I'm a kwami, and my name is Tikki. Let me explain."

Marinette was too freaked out to let the creature talk. She did what she always did when she felt in danger. "Mum! Dad!" she called.

Tikki flew through the glass without shattering it. "No, no, no!" Tikki cried. "I'm your friend, Marinette. You must trust me. You are the only one who can stop Stoneheart."

Marinette stared at Tikki and gently closed the hatch to her attic bedroom.

"I'm sorry if I scared you, but you have been chosen, Marinette," Tikki said.

"Chosen for what?" Marinette asked, a little breathlessly. "By who?"

"By someone who believes you have a good heart, Marinette, to be the superhero Paris needs. Those earrings aren't just earrings. They are ancient, powerful jewels called a Miraculous. By putting them on, you'll have special powers to defeat any evil that crosses your path."

Marinette's eyes widened and she stared at Tikki in disbelief. "There has to be some mistake," she said, hopelessly. "The only superpower I have is super-awkwardness!"

Tikki flew close to Marinette. "And yet, YOU are the chosen one, Marinette," she said, solemnly. "I know it's a lot to take in, but you need to learn fast if you are to defeat Stoneheart. There are some important things you need to know. Once transformed, the earrings will give you a superpower called Lucky Charm. You will also have a special yo-yo to help you do super things."

"Lucky Charm?" Marinette asked, feeling overwhelmed.

"Yes," Tikki smiled. "The superpower creates a lucky-charm object that you need at that exact

moment to save the day, but you must use it in a timely fashion," Tikki warned. "Five minutes after you use your superpower, you'll transform back into your normal self."

"But how can I? I mean, just me and a yo-yo against a giant supervillain?"

"You won't be alone. You'll have a partner, too, but you'll meet him soon enough."

Tikki swooped down to pick up the box and the red-and-black earrings that had been thrown at her moments ago. She handed them to Marinette. "Believe in yourself, Marinette. The Miraculous aren't given to just anyone. There is something special inside you. You can do this."

Marinette wasn't so sure.

CHAPTER FIVE

Transformation

*A*drien shielded his eyes as a burst of light filled his bedroom. When he lowered his arm, Adrien saw a small, black creature floating lifelessly in mid-air. He stared at the creature, utterly confused and at the same time completely fascinated. "No way!" he said, giving the sleepy creature a gentle poke. "You're like the genie in the lamp!"

At this, the little creature straightened up and folded his arms. He did not look amused.

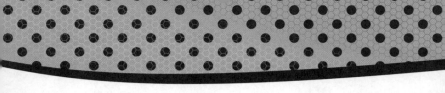

"The Genie? I met him once. So he grants wishes? Big. Deal. I'm way more personable," he swooped in circles around Adrien, showing off his long tail. "I'm Plagg. Got anything to eat?"

Before Adrien could answer, Plagg shot off around his bedroom, munching on anything he could land on. "Hey! Don't touch that!" Adrien wailed as Plagg tried to take a bite out of his football table.

"Ooh, shiny! Can you eat this?" Plagg set himself down on one of Adrien's full-sized arcade machines and tried to nibble the joystick. "Yuk! Apparently, you can't..."

As Plagg busied himself trying to chew on the buttons of Adrien's television remote, Adrien crawled up behind the little black creature and captured him in his hands. "I still don't know what you are doing here," Adrien demanded, breathlessly. "Care to explain a little?"

Plagg sighed. He was far more interested in

finding food than explaining his purpose in Adrien's bedroom. "Look, I'm a kwami. I grant powers. Yours is the power of destruction. It's called Cataclysm. Because you're kind of like a cat – I always liked that part. Get it?"

If Plagg was hoping that would be all it took to explain everything to Adrien, he was going to be disappointed. Adrien stared at Plagg and shook his head. "Nope."

Ignoring him, Plagg said, "Good. Now, got anything to eat around here? I'm starving!"

Adrien wanted to get to the bottom of this. The only things that ever happened to him were controlled to the very last detail by his dad. He had to be behind this. "My dad's pranking me, right?" he asked Plagg, before checking himself. "No, wait, it can't be my dad, he doesn't have a sense of humour."

Suddenly, Plagg forgot about his stomach and folded his arms. "Your father must never

know that I exist. Or anyone else for that matter."
Plagg knew that if he was ever going to get
Adrien to understand – and if he was ever going
to get any food – he had to explain who he was.
"You've been chosen, Adrien. You're going to be
a superhero."

Adrien stared at the little kwami feeling a
mixture of excitement and utter disbelief. Surely
the creature had made a mistake. "But I'm stuck
here. I never even get to go to school. What
good is a superhero who's imprisoned in his
own house?"

This didn't seem to bother Plagg. "No good
at all," he replied, cheerfully. "That's why it's all
going to change soon. If you are willing to change,
that is. You'll have a partner, a silver baton-thingy
and your superpower of Cataclysm, but the rest
is up to you."

Just then, Adrien felt something smooth and
cold in his hand. As he looked down he realised

he was holding a small, silver ring. It must have dropped out of the jewellery box when Plagg appeared.

He had a decision to make.

Marinette fixed the earrings into her ears and went over everything she had just learned from Tikki. She still wasn't at all sure she could do this, but if she really was the only one who could stop Stoneheart she had to at least try. "So, all I have to do is find the object where the whatchamacallit is hiding?"

Tikki sighed, patiently. "It's called an akuma. The akuma will have been sent to find Ivan and transform him into Stoneheart. It will be hiding inside an object. If Ivan lets the object go, the spell will be broken."

"Got it, and what about my charm thingy, again?" Marinette still felt like there was too

much information to process.

"It's called Lucky Charm, and it's your secret superpower. It will help you with whatever battles you have to face."

Marinette's shoulders slumped in defeat. "This is all going too fast, Tikki. I won't be able to pull this off."

Just an hour ago, Marinette was a normal schoolgirl. The biggest villain she had ever had to face was Chloé, and she couldn't even take her on without Alya's help. Who was she kidding?

Tikki fluttered close to Marinette's face, as though she could read her thoughts. "Trust yourself, Marinette," she said, kindly. "Just take a deep breath and say, 'Spots on!'"

"Spots on?" Marinette repeated, and before she knew it, the air around her had begun to fizz and sparkle. Marinette felt herself being lifted off the ground as Tikki disappeared inside the earrings. A spotted mask covered Marinette's eyes and, as she spun round, her clothes transformed into a sleek, red, all-in-one costume with the black spots of a ladybug. A yo-yo appeared on her hip just as she felt a burst of energy flow through her entire body. As Marinette gently returned to the floor of her bedroom, she felt stronger and more agile. She was aware of everything in her room, from the ticking of her bedside clock to the tiny draught coming through her closed bedroom window.

Marinette stared at herself in her bedroom mirror. "How does this thing come off?" she asked, desperately looking for a button or zipper on her new costume. "Tikki, if you can hear me, I want my normal clothes back!" Marinette felt ridiculous. She was dressed like a superhero, but still felt like a frightened little girl.

Marinette realised her computer was still showing the rolling news report on Stoneheart's

attack on the city. The police had not been able to stop him and he was still terrorising the streets of Paris. Worse still, the cameras had zoomed in to show that the police were not the only people on Stoneheart's trail. Alya was closing in on Stoneheart with only her bike and backpack for protection. Marinette's new best friend might be in danger. She had to do something.

Back in Adrien's bedroom, Adrien had slipped the silver cat's paw ring on his finger. It fitted perfectly, but the perfect accessory wasn't going to help him save Paris.

"Claws out," said Plagg as he absent-mindedly played with a toilet-roll tube. "That's what you have to say to transform, and—"

"Got it!" Adrien interrupted, excitedly. If he truly was going to be a superhero, he wanted to try it out as soon as possible.

"No, wait! I haven't finished explaining—"

"PLAGG, CLAWS OUT!" Adrien cried.

Before Plagg could finish, he had disappeared to become part of Adrien's superhero disguise. A cool, black supersuit replaced Adrien's jeans and shirt. A black mask covered his identity and on the tips of his gloves were sharp cat's claws. The silver baton Plagg had mentioned was fixed to his belt and he suddenly felt able to jump high and balance like a cat.

Once his transformation was complete, Adrien stood back and looked in the mirror. "Too cool," he said, admiring his new look. "Right, it's time to save Paris!"

CHAPTER SIX

Partners Collide

"**M**arinette, did you get home okay?" Sabine called to her daughter. The news of Stoneheart's attack had everyone in Paris on high alert and, although she was sure she had seen Marinette's bag in the hallway, Sabine hadn't actually seen her daughter since this morning.

"Marinette?" Sabine popped her head through the floor hatch of Marinette's attic bedroom. It was empty, although she could have

sworn she saw a flash of something red and black disappearing onto the roof terrace. She waited a moment before shaking her head and returning downstairs to the bakery. A supervillain on the loose had got her imagination running away with itself. "Tom? We'd better call the school."

Marinette paced the roof terrace as she worked out her next move. "Okay, so I have superpowers..." Even saying the words out loud felt utterly ridiculous. No one really had superpowers, did they? But here she was, wearing, she had to admit, a pretty cool supersuit, and tasked with defending Paris from a real-life supervillain.

She reached for the clip behind her and pulled out a ladybug spotted yo-yo. "And a super-yo-yo-thingy..." Tikki had explained that her yo-yo could do incredible things, but to Marinette it just looked like a child's toy.

Without thinking, Marinette fired the yo-yo

high above her. It shot like an arrow to the top of a nearby building and neatly wrapped itself around a stone gargoyle.

Great start, Marinette sighed. How was she supposed to get it down? She tugged at the string, but instead of loosening it, the strength of the yo-yo catapulted Marinette into the air. Soon she was soaring high above the streets of Paris in total panic, with only the string of her yo-yo to keep her from falling to certain death. "WAHHHH!"

Marinette was hurtling back to Earth when she spotted a figure, clad all in black, balancing on a beam below her. There was nothing she could do, they were going to hit!

As Marinette collided with the figure, the string of her yo-yo wrapped around them and left the pair dangling in the air just inches from the pavement. Despite her transformation, Marinette still felt like the clumsy schoolgirl she knew she really was.

"Hey there!" said the figure, who Marinette could now see was a boy. A superhero boy. "Nice of you to drop in."

"I'm sorry," Marinette blushed. "I didn't do it on purpose."

The boy smoothly wriggled out of the yo-yo's string and landed cat-like on the ground. "I bet you're the partner my kwami told me about. I'm..." the boy thought for a second. "I'm Cat Noir," he said, as though testing it out for the first time. "Yeah, Cat Noir. And you are?"

Marinette was only half listening. She was trying to get her yo-yo to untangle itself. "I'm Ma—." She stopped, remembering what Tikki had told her. No one could know who she really was, her identity had to remain a secret. Luckily, her yo-yo was there to change the subject as it flipped back into her hand via Cat Noir's head. "I'm madly clumsy, sorry," she said, apologetically.

"No sweat, clumsy girl," Cat Noir rubbed the mop of blond hair on top of his head and flashed her a smile. "I'm learning the ropes, too."

Marinette smiled back. So, this was the partner Tikki had told her about. Having a partner was going to make this superhero thing a lot easier and Cat Noir seemed to know what he was doing, even if he was a little overconfident. Surely no one could learn they were a superhero, transform and be that sure of themselves all in one day?

Before they had a chance to talk more, the ground began to shake and a building collapsed. It had to be Stoneheart.

Cat Noir pulled out a small silver baton with a green paw print at the top. Although he hadn't given Plagg the time to explain what it could do, Cat Noir was quickly learning how to use it. With a flick of his wrist, the baton extended into a giant pole and Cat Noir used it to vault onto

the rooftops.

Marinette gasped. Cat Noir seemed to be so much more comfortable with his powers than she ever felt she could be. "Where are you going?!" she called, panicked.

Cat Noir balanced on the building with ease and grinned. "To save Paris, right?"

Marinette felt as though her legs were going to buckle beneath her. She pulled her shoulders back and breathed. "Trust yourself, believe in yourself," she repeated the mantra Tikki had given her earlier that day when all this could still have been a bad dream.

Marinette felt the yo-yo in her hand and began to understand what it could do. She realised she could control it if she put her mind to it and began to wind it deftly behind her before firing it towards the building Cat Noir had just leapt from. There was no turning back now.

She was going to save Paris.

CHAPTER SEVEN

Stoneheart Attacks

*D*espite being under attack from a supervillain made of pure stone, nothing stopped the Collège Françoise Dupont soccer team, or their star player Kim, from getting in their regular training practice.

The team had just finished up and were preparing to leave the stadium when a thunderous noise made them freeze. Stoneheart bounded onto the roof of the stands and roared, "KIM!" He had grown even larger and his growl echoed

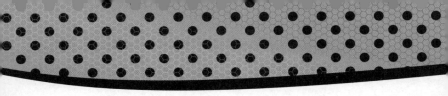

around the stadium in a deafening wave.

Kim was too afraid to move as his teammates scattered. What did this terrifying creature want with him?

"So," Stoneheart boomed. "Who's the wuss now?"

Stoneheart soared into the stadium in a single leap, as Kim's stomach lurched. It was Ivan. The monstrous stone villain that had been terrorising Paris was a boy in his class. A boy he had made fun of with a stupid, silly note.

Kim began to flee as Stoneheart landed, focused on revenge. Kim wasn't going anywhere fast, his legs seemed to crumble with fear. Stoneheart had his chance. He stretched out a boulder-shaped arm as Kim shut his eyes in terror, but something was stopping Stoneheart. A silver pole formed a barrier between Stoneheart and Kim, just long enough for Kim to scramble to his feet and flee.

In his place stood Cat Noir, fearless in the face of the gigantic stone creature. "Hey," he said, casually flipping his baton onto his shoulder. "It's not very nice to pick on people who are smaller than you."

Stoneheart's eyes glowed with rage. "You must be talking about yourself!" he boomed, landing a heavy stone hand on the spot Cat Noir had just swiftly exited.

Cat Noir leapt and pounced around the slow and cumbersome Stoneheart, dodging the swipes and stamps that could crush him instantly. With each return blow Cat Noir landed, Stoneheart grew bigger and stronger. "Where are you, partner?" Cat Noir called, hoping that his new partner was somewhere nearby.

Hawk Moth laughed and raised his arms to drink in the chaos he had created. "Everything is

going according to plan," he said with an evil smile. "The Miraculouses have been activated and here come the superheroes to save the day. Now my supervillain will destroy them and their Miraculouses will be mine. Nothing is going to stop me now!"

Unfortunately, the one thing that had the power to stop Hawk Moth was standing on the stadium roof, watching in fear as Cat Noir struggled to dodge Stoneheart's blows.

"I can't," Marinette breathed heavily. "I'm not going to be able to do it."

Suddenly, Stoneheart ripped the goal from the pitch and threw it at Cat Noir. With his feline reflexes, Cat Noir dodged, sending the goal hurtling towards... Alya.

Alya had tracked Stoneheart to the stadium and was not about to miss her chance to film and photograph real superheroes in action. Marinette's heart surged as she saw her friend in danger.

Cat Noir threw his baton, it spun and flipped landing perfectly to form a barrier between the flying goal and Alya's hiding spot. But without his baton, Cat Noir was vulnerable. Stoneheart took his chance and grabbed Cat Noir in his giant, rocky hand.

Marinette stood helplessly and watched. Her feet seemed to be glued to the roof of the stadium. "What are you waiting for?" a familiar voice called. It was Alya. She had spotted Marinette. "The world is watching you!"

Did Alya know it was Marinette? Was the world really watching? How long could Cat Noir stay in the grip of that terrible monster?

Believe in yourself. Marinette gripped her yo-yo and felt a surge of confidence flow through her. This was it. It was her time. She jumped,

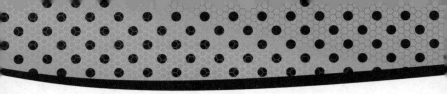

catapulting the string of her yo-yo around Stoneheart's feet. As she landed perfectly on the pitch, she tugged the yo-yo's string, sending Stoneheart flying and releasing Cat Noir. "Animal cruelty?" she quipped. "How shameful."

As Stoneheart struggled, Marinette ran to Cat Noir. "I'm sorry I took so long."

"That's okay." Cat Noir sprang to his feet. "Now, let's kick his rocky behind!"

Marinette grabbed Cat Noir by his tail. Fighting wasn't going to stop Stoneheart and she had to make Cat Noir understand. "Haven't you noticed? He gets bigger and stronger after every attack. We have to do something different."

Cat Noir stopped. His partner was right. Without a plan they were in danger of losing the battle. "Different how?"

Marinette thought hard. "I don't know," she admitted. She had only just become a superhero, and she needed time to think.

CHAPTER EIGHT

Superpowers!

Time to think was a luxury Cat Noir and Marinette did not have. Stoneheart was starting to recover from his fall and Marinette still didn't have a plan.

"If you don't know, then I think I have the answer," Cat Noir said with a glint in his eye. "Let's use our superpowers!"

Neither of them had used their superpowers before. Tikki had carefully explained to Marinette that her power of creation, Lucky Charm, could

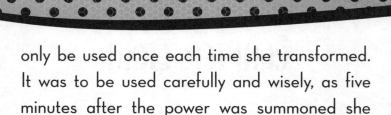

only be used once each time she transformed. It was to be used carefully and wisely, as five minutes after the power was summoned she would transform back into a regular girl.

Marinette tried to stop Cat Noir, but before she could even take a breath, he had turned to face Stoneheart. "Cataclysm!" Cat Noir shouted. The ring on Cat Noir's finger shone and a tremendous power surged through his hands.

"Apparently I have the power of destruction," Cat Noir said, more impressed with himself than Marinette was. "Watch!"

"No! Don't do that!" Marinette cried as Cat Noir tapped a goal post and watched as it turned to dust.

Excited by the power he thought he now possessed, Cat Noir scampered towards Stoneheart. "Time to rumble, soon-to-be-rubble!" he quipped as he landed by Stoneheart's feet. But as he placed his clawed hand on the monster, expecting him to crumble into dust like the goal post, nothing happened. For a moment, Stoneheart stared at Cat Noir as both of them expected something more to happen. However, Stoneheart soon got tired and proceeded to kick Cat Noir the length of the pitch.

"I guess I only get one shot at using my power," Cat Noir said, rubbing his head for the second time that day. Being a superhero was fun, but he wasn't sure how he was going to explain all the bumps and bruises to his dad.

"You realise you've now only got five minutes before you change back?" Marinette scolded. "Didn't your kwami teach you anything?"

Cat Noir smiled charmingly and stretched. "I guess I was kind of overexcited about my new life to listen to the rule book."

Marinette couldn't help smiling, too. Cat Noir was brave, but reckless. She was starting to understand why they were partners. It was going to be her job to do things logically, while Cat Noir took all the risks.

"Then it's up to me," Marinette declared, more confidently than she could have ever imagined just a few hours ago. "Lucky Charm!" she cried.

Marinette's yo-yo shot a stream of glittering hearts into the air, which then transformed into the object that was going to help her defeat Stoneheart. As it fluttered to the ground, Marinette was confused. "A diver's wetsuit?"

Stoneheart was slowly trudging from his side of the stadium to where Cat Noir and Marinette were standing. She had to think fast. "My kwami told me we have to destroy the object where the akuma is hiding – it's what's turned Ivan into that monster. We find the object, we defeat the monster." Marinette stared at Stoneheart as he got closer and closer. "His right hand!" Marinette cried. "He never opens it! That must be where the akuma is hiding."

"So, what's your plan?" asked Cat Noir, ready to help, but uncertain as to how.

Marinette scanned the stadium as quickly as she could, taking in everything that could help her.

She knew what she had to do.

"Don't resist," Marinette said to Cat Noir as she wrapped the string of her yo-yo around his legs. She picked up the wetsuit and grabbed a water hose that was lying nearby. In a flash she had secured the nozzle of the hose inside the wetsuit. *I hope this works*, Marinette thought to herself.

Cat Noir gulped. He didn't like not being in control. "Trust me," Marinette said as she whipped Cat Noir into the air and propelled him towards Stoneheart.

Stoneheart caught Cat Noir with his left

hand. *Stage one, complete!* thought Marinette as she launched herself into the air. "Catch me if you can!" she called. Stoneheart had no choice but to drop the black paper ball he had been carrying. The akuma's object was out of his grasp at last, but Cat Noir and Marinette were not. "Alya!" Marinette called. "The tap!"

Alya had been watching the battle from her hiding place at the side of the pitch. She never dreamed she might become part of the action, but here she was, being given instructions by the most incredible superhero she had ever seen. She spotted a tap a little way off and ran to it as fast as she could. As she turned it on, the water hose that was attached bulged with water.

Soon, the wetsuit Marinette was holding had filled with water to the point where Stoneheart couldn't keep his hand closed any longer. Marinette jumped free and crushed the black paper ball under her foot as she landed.

Marinette felt incredible as the akuma fluttered away into the sky.

Stoneheart's supervillain exterior crumbled away in a cloud of black smoke, releasing Cat Noir and leaving Ivan dazed and confused, wondering what had just happened.

Cat Noir blinked. "That girl is awesome!" he laughed, totally impressed with the clumsy girl he had met earlier that day. "Crazy awesome!"

Ladybug

Marinette

Adrien

Cat Noir

Alya

Tom & Sabine

Nino &
Chloé

Hawk Moth

CHAPTER NINE

Just Call Me Ladybug

"**Y**ou were incredible, Miss, erm... Buglady," Cat Noir stuttered. "You really did it!"

Marinette smiled, amused to see Cat Noir lost for words for once. "We both did it, partner," she said. The two brand-new superheroes bumped fists and revelled in their success, but the alarm on Cat Noir's ring signalled danger. He was going to change back at any moment.

"You'd better get going," Marinette warned. "Our identities must be kept secret."

Cat Noir bowed extravagantly. "Farewell, my lady. Let's do this again soon, okay?" he grinned at Marinette and scampered into the distance.

"Marinette rolled her eyes. "Not too soon, I hope." She admitted to herself that saving Paris from a giant stone supervillain had been kind of fun, although she preferred monsters who stayed in fairy tales.

Just then, Marinette realised she was holding the balled-up piece of paper the akuma had been hiding in. She smoothed it out and read the note aloud. "You haven't even got the guts to tell Mylène you like her, wuss." So that was it. Ivan liked a girl in their class called Mylène, and Marinette was willing to bet her dad's bakery on the fact that Mylène liked Ivan, too. But somehow, the boy who most students at the school were afraid of because of his size, was actually too shy to talk to the girl he liked.

"Kim wrote it," Ivan admitted, as he watched Marinette reading the note. "He's always making fun of me."

Marinette sat down next to Ivan on the grass. "You know, you shouldn't get so bent out of shape about all this, Ivan. There's no shame in telling someone you like them."

Ivan stared at Marinette wide-eyed. "Hey, how do you know my name?"

In that moment, Marinette had forgotten who she was meant to be, and who she definitely wasn't meant to be. Luckily, Alya appeared and was so busy filming Marinette with her phone she couldn't help but butt in.

"Uncanny! Amazing! Spectacular!" Alya cried. "Are you going to be protecting Paris from now on? How did you get your powers? Were you bitten by a radioactive ladybug? Oh, I've got a ton of questions to ask you, Miss..."

Marinette began to walk away from Alya's

camera, scared her identity might be revealed. She paused, knowing it was time to give herself a name.

"Ladybug," she said, smiling. "Just call me Ladybug."

⚽ ⚽ ⚽

Now that Stoneheart had been defeated, Paris was in celebration mode. What other city on the planet could boast having not one, but two superhero protectors? As she watched the news on her computer screen, Marinette hugged her knees and beamed with pride. "I did it, Tikki!" she said.

Tikki snuggled into Marinette. "You see? You were up to it all along!" Tikki said, proud of Marinette.

Marinette couldn't believe she was a superhero. Not only that, a superhero with superpowers. A superhero with superpowers who saved people! At that moment she felt like nothing could burst her bubble.

"... and so we will be organising a big celebration in honour of our city's new protectors, Ladybug and Cat Noir."

Adrien watched the news on the edge of his sofa in front of the giant TV in his bedroom, but it wasn't the news of a celebration in Cat Noir's honour that had Adrien excited. "Ladybug!" he gasped. "Her name's Ladybug!"

Ever since Adrien had changed back, all he could think about was his amazing partner and he would have carried on thinking about her had he not been interrupted by a furious-looking Plagg. "Eww! What is this?" Plagg asked, holding up an ice-cream sundae.

"My personal chef made all this," Adrien replied, gesturing to the table in front of them,

laid out with trays full of gourmet food.

"If you want me to get my energy back after a transformation, I need to eat something more delicate," Plagg said, unimpressed by the feast.

Adrien looked at Plagg suspiciously. "Okay, what do you want?"

CHAPTER TEN

Stone Statues

*H*igh above the streets of Paris, at the very top of the Eiffel Tower, a strange black moth landed and beat its wings for a moment or two before multiplying into hundreds of moths, spreading across Paris in every direction. The akumas began to land on unsuspecting Parisians, and as they did, the innocent people turned into stone beings, as still as statues.

"Oh my!" Marinette heard her mother gasp as Marinette washed the dishes after dinner. Sabine was watching the news in their living room and Marinette's heart sank like a stone as she watched the report over her shoulder. Hundreds of people all over the city were being turned into stone beings just like Ivan, as small black moths landed on them. The only difference being that instead of roaming the streets looking for revenge, the stone beings were rooted to the spot like statues.

Marinette ran back to her room. "Tikki!" Marinette called as she switched on the computer screen. "What's going on? I thought we defeated Stoneheart?"

Tikki watched the news and dropped the cookie she was munching on. "Did you capture the akuma?" Tikki asked with a serious look on her face.

Marinette shook her head. She didn't

understand. "What's capturing the akuma got to do with anything?" Marinette had done everything Tikki had asked of her, hadn't she? Ivan was back to normal. Why was this happening?

"An akuma can multiply, that's why it must be captured," Tikki explained, patiently. "If Ivan's emotions become negative again, his akuma will find him and turn him back into Stoneheart. He'll then be able to control these other stone beings and bring them to life to serve as his army!"

Marinette stared at Tikki in disbelief. How could this happen? How could she have gotten it so wrong? Moments ago she was feeling on top of the world, and now everything had turned to dust. It was all her fault.

"You see, Tikki!" Marinette cried, hopelessly. "I'm not cut out to be a superhero! I'm only going to keep messing up."

But Tikki was a positive little kwami. She had

seen things far worse than this and she knew Marinette had great power within her. "Stay calm," she said, kindly, as Marinette turned away. "It was only your first time. You're going to go back and capture Stoneheart's akuma, and be successful!"

Marinette rounded on Tikki. She liked the little creature, but at that moment she hated herself and needed someone to take it out on. "I told you, I can't! I'm clumsy. I create disaster all the time. I'll only make things worse, for me, for you, for everyone. Cat Noir will be better off without me. I'm quitting."

As she said the words Marinette felt equally relieved and devastated. As Ladybug, Marinette was confident, in control, capable of anything. As Marinette, she felt as though the world would be better off if she didn't get out of bed in the morning.

"I'm sorry, Marinette," Tikki said, softly. "But

Cat Noir can't do anything without you."

Marinette turned round, confused. "I don't understand."

"Only you have the power to capture akumas and repair the damage done by supervillains. It's part of your gift."

As she walked over to her dressing table to pick up the little black jewellery box she had been given earlier that day, Marinette sighed. "If Cat Noir can't do anything without Ladybug, then find another Ladybug."

Marinette fiddled with the clasps of her ladybug earrings.

"No, don't!" Tikki warned, but it was too late. As the earrings came off, Tikki vanished.

Marinette sighed. She liked Tikki a lot, but it would be better for everyone if she found someone else to protect Paris. She placed the jewellery box in her dresser drawer and sank to her knees.

In his secret lair, Hawk Moth was feeling rejuvenated after Stoneheart's defeat. His akuma had done its job and had fluttered back to its master. "Ivan has a sensitive heart," he smiled. "It won't be long before anger and sadness strike him again. Then he and the stone beings will come alive!"

He banged his silver cane on the floor, sending his moths fluttering here and there. "We'll see how long you stay hidden, Ladybug and Cat Noir. Once I have your Miraculouses you will be powerless against me. Everyone will be powerless against me. I will have ABSOLUTE POWER!"

CHAPTER ELEVEN

A Reluctant Hero

The following morning, nothing had changed. The stone beings were still frozen, although they had now been surrounded by police. No one knew when, or if, they would come to life and all Paris could do was sit and wait.

Marinette got ready for school as usual. She was determined to leave what happened yesterday behind her. Despite the total exhilaration she felt as she battled Stoneheart, she had ultimately let everyone down by letting

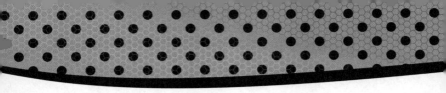

the akuma go free. Whoever transformed into Ladybug had the responsibility to de-evilise akumas, and Marinette just didn't feel like she had the strength to be that person.

She sighed as she walked past her dresser and glanced at the drawer that contained the ladybug earrings. Slowly she pulled the little black jewellery box out and slipped it into her purse.

She had an idea that she was certain would solve everything.

Like virtually every other family in Paris, Tom and Sabine Dupain-Cheng had their television fixed on the news channel. Marinette could barely swallow her cereal as the reporter relayed the latest information.

"Paris is relying on our new guardian angels, Ladybug and Cat Noir, to save us all. Our lives depend on them."

"Listen, I know how upsetting and scary this

is," Marinette's dad put a strong arm around her shoulders. "But we've got two superheroes looking after Paris and the best way to help them is to show them we're not scared, because we trust them."

Marinette loved the way her dad had faith in Ladybug and Cat Noir. More than anything she wanted to make her parents proud. "But what if Ladybug fails?" Marinette asked, genuinely wanting to know the answer.

"Then I'll come and save you!" Tom pulled a freshly baked baguette from the counter and used it as a sword. "Super-baker to the rescue!"

Marinette giggled and hugged her dad goodbye. If she'd been any other girl, this would have been enough to make all her worries disappear – as it was, Marinette had to solve the bigger problems herself.

Adrien woke up in his luxurious bedroom, surrounded by everything a teenage boy could wish for, but there was only one thing on his mind. Escape.

Yesterday he had transformed into Cat Noir and helped to save Paris from a supervillain. Today he felt as though he could do anything, and right now all he wanted to do was go to school. He glanced at the cat's paw ring on his finger and smiled.

"You're such a strange kid," said Plagg, floating alongside Adrien as he sprinted away from his house towards the Collège Françoise Dupont. "Who would want to be at school when you could be at home all day?" Plagg was an ancient creature, and of all the people he had ever met, Adrien was the most puzzling.

"You don't get it, Plagg," Adrien said breathlessly, not slowing his pace. "I've had enough of being shut up at home by my father.

I want to meet people and make friends. Go to a normal school, just like everyone else."

Plagg rolled his eyes and let out a dramatic cry. "I think I'm feeling weak..." he said, stopping suddenly.

Although they had only known each other for twenty-four hours, Adrien already knew Plagg's little tricks. He took a triangle of Camembert cheese out of his shoulder bag. "You know what's strange? The fact that all you eat is this rotten, stinky cheese." He handed it to Plagg, who took a bite greedily. "And I have to smell like rotten, stinky cheese twenty-four seven. That's strange."

Plagg swallowed and grinned. "If you want to change into a superhero then stinky cheese is the deal, my friend."

Alya handed Marinette her phone. It was showing a blog post with an extremely familiar

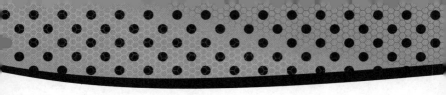

character starring in the main picture. "I call it LadyBlog!" Alya said, proudly. "How cool is that? You should see how many views I've had since I posted the video I took yesterday."

Instead of being flattered by Alya's adoration for Ladybug, Marinette despaired. "Why do you trust Ladybug? There are so many of those stone beings out there and only one of her."

"She's going to handle them," Alya said, confidently.

"What if she's not really cut out to be a superhero? Even if everyone around her keeps telling her she is?"

"What are you talking about?" Alya asked, laughing. Then she stopped and looked at Marinette for a moment. "Wait!" she said, adjusting her glasses. "I know what this is." Marinette panicked. Had her professional superhero-hunter friend worked out her identity already? "You're scared." Alya placed a comforting hand on Marinette's shoulders as Marinette breathed a sigh of relief. "Don't worry. Ladybug is going to protect us all. I've seen her with my own two eyes. She's amazing. I believe in her."

Marinette's heart lifted for just a moment. If Alya believed in Ladybug, then maybe Marinette could do it after all?

CHAPTER TWELVE

Stay Positive!

*I*van sat miserably in the hallway as his classmates bombarded him with questions.

"Are you seriously saying you don't remember anything?" asked one classmate.

"You were going totally ballistic. It was so cool," added another.

"Yeah, you were seriously out to crush me, dude!" said Kim. He wanted answers. As Stoneheart, Ivan had totalled half of Paris trying to find him.

"I'm sorry," Ivan said, shaking his head in disbelief. "I wasn't myself." At that moment, he glanced up and spotted Mylène staring at him. Ivan couldn't bear to imagine what she thought of him now. As if she could read his mind, Mylène looked away and walked quickly to the girls' bathroom.

Ivan sighed and looked down. He couldn't take one more comment.

Unfortunately, Chloé had other ideas. "Once a monster, always a monster," her shrill voice echoed in Ivan's head. Maybe she was right? Ivan stood up and stomped through the wall of classmates, sending every negative emotion he was feeling to Hawk Moth and Stoneheart's akuma.

Alya and Marinette had been watching silently, until now. "Chloé, how could you say that to Ivan?" asked Alya, angrily. "You're the real Stoneheart, here."

Chloé giggled. "So I'm the one who went on a rampage through Paris, am I?" she asked the group, then turned her gaze on Alya. "Just because your footage of those lame superheroes got on TV doesn't mean you get to be all high and mighty."

Alya flushed and clenched her fists.

"Watch out, everyone!" Chloé teased. "She's going to split her underwear and turn into a muscly monster!"

Alya was so angry she couldn't get her mouth to work. Luckily, something far more interesting grabbed Chloé's attention.

Adrien Agreste had just walked into school.

"Adri-kins!" Chloé squealed, throwing her arms around his neck. The remaining students who hadn't already made it into class started to whisper and giggle. Adrien Agreste, the famous model, was at their school!

Marinette, however, had more important

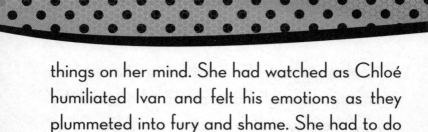

things on her mind. She had watched as Chloé humiliated Ivan and felt his emotions as they plummeted into fury and shame. She had to do something to help him, or there was a danger he would turn into Stoneheart again.

Marinette found Ivan slumped against his locker. His headphones were on full blast, blocking out the world. Everyone else was either in class or trying to get a glimpse of Adrien Agreste. She crouched down beside him and placed a friendly hand on his arm. "You know," she began, as Ivan removed his headphones. "You should just tell Mylène how you feel."

Ivan blushed and cleared his throat. "I... I don't know what you're talking about."

"Come on," Marinette said, smiling encouragingly. "I've seen the way you look at her! And I'm pretty sure she likes you, too." Marinette knew that if she could make Ivan happy, Hawk Moth's akuma had no chance of turning him back into Stoneheart. And what could make him happier than uniting him with Mylène?

"I'm no good with words," Ivan admitted.

"Who needs words?" Marinette wasn't going to be beaten. "You could draw her a picture, or send her flowers."

Ivan looked thoughtful. "I could write her a song, I guess."

"That's a GREAT idea! What girl wouldn't want a song written especially for her? Go for it, Ivan and... stay positive!"

Adrien walked through the corridors of his new school with Chloé hanging off his arm, signing autographs as he went.

"This is our classroom, Adri-kins," simpered Chloé. "And this is your seat. I saved it for you, right in front of me!"

Adrien looked around the classroom. It was about half the size of his bedroom and smelled a little of chalk dust, but it contained the one thing he had never really had before. Kids his own age.

"Hi, I'm Adrien," he said, cheerfully, to the boy sitting in the seat next to his.

The boy eyed him suspiciously. "So you're friends with Chloé, huh?" he said, unimpressed.

Adrien nodded, confused. Was being friends with Chloé such a bad thing? As if to answer his question he turned to see Chloé and her friend Sabrina putting a sticky glob of chewing gum on the bank of seats by the window. "Hey, what are you doing?" Adrien jumped up. He might not have been to school before, but he knew a nasty prank when he saw one.

"The brats who sat here yesterday need to be taught a lesson," Chloé explained. "I'm just demanding a bit of respect, that's all."

Adrien frowned. "Do you think that's really

necessary?" he asked. He'd known Chloé a long time, but he didn't realise how unpleasant she could be. He bent down to try and remove the sticky mess while Chloé giggled.

Just outside the classroom, Marinette had another important job to do. "Alya, you'd like to be a superhero, right?"

"Totally! I'm not scared of anyone! Why?"

"Oh, no reason." Marinette quietly opened her purse and held the black jewellery box in her hand. She knew what she had to do was for the best. Swiftly she placed the box inside Alya's shoulder bag. Now Alya would find the earrings and Tikki would turn her into Ladybug and she'd be ten times the superhero Marinette could ever be.

Marinette was feeling pretty pleased with herself until she stepped into the classroom. The new boy everyone had been going crazy over was kneeling by her desk putting chewing gum on her seat. "Hey! What do you think you are doing?" she demanded.

Adrien couldn't think what to say. If he told the truth he would betray his one and only friend in the entire school.

Chloé and Sabrina started to cackle, leaving Marinette to come to her own conclusion. "Okay, you three, very funny."

"You don't understand!" Adrien protested. "I was trying to take it off."

Marinette looked between him and her worst enemy. "You're friends with Chloé, right?" she said, accusingly.

Adrien ruffled his hair. Why did people keep saying that? Marinette placed a sheet of tissue over the gum and sat miserably next to Alya. "He looks familiar," she whispered to Alya who was frantically swiping through her phone. She handed it to Marinette to show her image after image of Adrien posing for fashion lines and aftershave. "Of course!" Marinette gasped. "He's the son of my favourite fashion designer, Gabriel Agreste!"

"Daddy's boy, teen supermodel AND friends with Chloé!" Alya grimaced. "Forget him."

Adrien stared down at his desk. His first day was not going as planned. The boy sitting next to him was confused. "Why didn't you just tell them it was Chloé?" he asked.

Adrien sighed. "I've known Chloé since I was a little kid. I couldn't throw her under the bus. She is literally the only friend I have."

The boy smiled and held out his hand. "I'm Nino," he said. "I think it's time you made some new friends."

CHAPTER THIRTEEN

Stoneheart Returns

Mylène was still hiding in the girls' bathroom. She couldn't bear the nasty way Chloé, Kim and the others were talking to Ivan and she had a horrible, sinking feeling that somehow all this was her fault.

Ivan and Mylène had been friends for a long time. They liked the same bands and loved hanging out at the skate park together, but Ivan was just so shy. Mylène never really knew if he liked her as a friend, or something more.

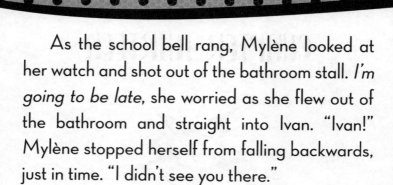

As the school bell rang, Mylène looked at her watch and shot out of the bathroom stall. *I'm going to be late*, she worried as she flew out of the bathroom and straight into Ivan. "Ivan!" Mylène stopped herself from falling backwards, just in time. "I didn't see you there."

Ivan looked at Mylène and suddenly felt overwhelmingly nervous. He had taken Marinette's advice and written Mylène a song. The lyrics were scribbled on a piece of paper he had torn out of his school book. He pulled his phone out of his pocket. It was ready to go with a backing track for the song. "I, er, wrote this for you," Ivan stumbled. He couldn't be sure, but he thought he saw Mylène smile a little. Maybe, just maybe, this was going to work.

Ivan pressed play on his phone and suddenly the air was filled with the deafening roar of one of Ivan's favourite rock bands. Ivan took a deep breath, closed his eyes and began to sing the special lyrics he had written.

However, singing wasn't quite what came out of Ivan's mouth. Ivan's voice was deafeningly scary and Mylène couldn't understand what he was saying. As his voice turned into a scream, she couldn't take it any more.

When Ivan opened his eyes, he realised Mylène wasn't standing in front of him anymore. He heard her footsteps as she ran away down the corridor.

Stopping the music, Ivan felt ashamed and humiliated. What had he done wrong? Was the music too loud? Were the lyrics too soppy? He looked at the piece of paper with his lyrics on and screwed it up into a tight ball. Throwing his phone on the floor in frustration, Ivan slumped, his head in his hands, never imagining anything could feel as bad as this.

"This is the moment we have been waiting for!" Hawk Moth cried, as he felt Ivan's negative emotions rising up again. "This is your chance, evil akuma." Hawk Moth released Stoneheart's akuma into the air. "You know the way. Track down your prey and evilise him!"

The akuma fluttered high above the streets of Paris and it wasn't long before it followed the trail of bad feelings to where Ivan cowered.

Landing perfectly on Ivan's screwed-up lyrics, the akuma reawakened Stoneheart, reconnecting him with Hawk Moth once again.

"This is your second chance, Stoneheart," Hawk Moth spoke directly to Ivan. "This time you have extra help. No one will stop you from capturing Mylène. Just remember that I will need something in return. Bring me the ladybug earrings and the cat's paw ring."

As he stood up, Ivan transformed once again into Stoneheart, and as he did, each of the stone beings around Paris began to wake up, terrorising neighbourhoods and pledging their loyalty to Stoneheart.

Unaware of Ivan's transformation, Adrien, Marinette and the rest of their classmates were beginning morning lessons. Adrien looked around the classroom. He'd finally made it! Here he was sitting in a nice, normal school surrounded by lots of nice, normal kids. Or so he thought.

At that moment, Stoneheart crashed into the classroom, taking out half the wall and covering the desks with rubble. "Mylène!" Stoneheart roared, scanning the rows of desks. He scooped Mylène up in his giant, rocky hand, still holding the screwed-up lyrics.

Struggling to get free, Mylène cried. "Let go of me, Ivan!"

"I'm not Ivan any more. I'm Stoneheart!"

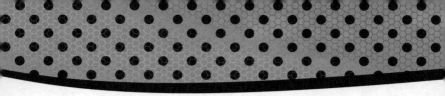

Stoneheart boomed.

Mylène stared at the stone beast. Was Ivan really gone? "Why are you doing this?"

"So we can be together!" Stoneheart replied, turning to take his prize away. But something made him stop. A shrill, whining voice hit his ears and filled him with even more anger.

Chloé was cowering under her desk, desperately trying to call the mayor's office to talk to her father.

Stoneheart felt the shame Ivan had felt when Chloé had belittled him in front of the whole class and his chest filled with rage. With his free hand, Stoneheart grabbed Chloé and jumped through the classroom wall onto the street below.

CHAPTER FOURTEEN

Spots Back On!

*A*lya couldn't believe her luck. Just a day after setting up her Ladybug blog, she was about to have front-row seats for Ladybug and Cat Noir's next rescue mission. She had just finished filming Stoneheart on her phone when she turned to her friend and said, "Come on, let's follow him."

Marinette had a different plan. She peeked out from behind her desk. "You go. I'm going to find myself a safe place to hide."

When Marinette transformed into Ladybug she was able to do incredible things. With Cat Noir by her side she had already defeated Stoneheart once before, but today, as plain old Marinette, she just couldn't do it.

"You're going to miss Ladybug in action!" Alya pleaded.

Marinette grabbed Alya's bag, knowing that the ladybug earrings were inside, and thrust it at her. "You and Ladybug will both be better off without me."

Alya shrugged. "If you say so." To Marinette's horror, Alya sprinted out of the classroom, leaving her bag behind. Alya had her trusty phone to capture all the action, her bag was just going to slow her down.

"Wait!" Marinette threw Alya's bag over her shoulder and ran to follow her friend.

Adrien sighed as he put his school books back in his locker. "My first day of school and I don't even make it past roll call," he moaned, as Plagg swooped out of his jacket.

"A day off?" Plagg asked, excitedly. "That's what I'm talking about!" But before Adrien's kwami could get too comfortable, Adrien showed he had other ideas.

"Nope, we've got homework to do," Adrien said, with a glint in his eye. Unlike Marinette, seeing Stoneheart rampaging through the school meant only one thing to Adrien – it was time to become Cat Noir and save Paris once again.

"Plagg, CLAWS OUT!"

Stoneheart stomped through the streets, keeping a tight grip on Mylène and Chloé. Despite being captured by a supervillain, Chloé couldn't keep herself from talking. "You have NO IDEA who you are dealing with," she wailed. "My daddy, the mayor, will summon the police, the army, the entire cavalry!"

"And don't forget the superheroes!" Cat Noir leapt from the sky, landing a blow on Stoneheart with his baton. Stoneheart took the blow and grew bigger. Cat Noir winced. How had he forgotten that Stoneheart grew with every hit he took? "Sorry, my bad!" he said, sheepishly.

"Superhero?" Chloé whined. "Super-incompetent don't you mean?"

Suddenly the ground began to shake with the rhythmic pounding of dozens of pairs of stone feet. "You wanted the cavalry?" laughed Stoneheart. "Well here it comes!"

Stone beings ran from every direction and surrounded Cat Noir. "Seize him!" Stoneheart commanded and the stone beings obeyed, swiping and grabbing at Cat Noir as he leaped and dodged their huge, rocky hands.

Stoneheart took his opportunity and left his stone soldiers to fight Cat Noir. "Where are we going?" Mylène asked. Although she was afraid, somehow, she knew Stoneheart wouldn't hurt her.

"To deliver a message. Then we'll be able to be together forever," Stoneheart replied.

Chloé scoffed. She wasn't used to being pushed around. "Urgh, all this lovey-dovey stuff is making me sick."

"Don't worry, I'm going to take care of you, too," Stoneheart said, menacingly, and for the first time in her life Chloé felt genuinely afraid.

As the fight between Cat Noir and the stone beings raged on, Cat Noir was beginning to wonder where his partner was. "If you can hear me, Ladybug, I could do with a little help!" Cat Noir dodged and weaved as the stone beings

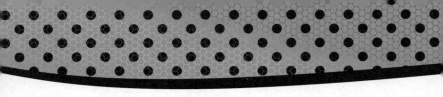

stomped and swiped at him, throwing anything they could find his way.

Meanwhile, Alya had found the perfect spot to film the battle on her phone, behind a dumpster bin. "Where is she?" Alya wondered, scanning the rooftops for any sign of Ladybug. Cat Noir was great and seemed to be doing okay, but she really needed Ladybug for her blog.

Ladybug was nowhere to be seen, because Marinette was still too frightened to transform into her. Finally catching up with Alya, Marinette was horrified by what she saw. Cat Noir was bravely battling the stone beings all by himself, but he couldn't do it alone for much longer.

One of the stone beings picked up a car as though it weighed nothing at all and launched it at Cat Noir. Cat Noir's reflexes were too quick for the lumbering beings and he managed to dodge out of the way, sending the car hurtling towards Alya's dumpster.

Luckily, Cat Noir threw his baton just in time to deflect the car's path, leaving Alya trapped, but unhurt. Now the stone beings saw their opportunity – Cat Noir was without his baton! One of the beings grabbed him and this time there was no escape.

Marinette watched, rooted to the spot, still holding Alya's bag. Her best friend was trapped and her partner had been captured. She had to do something! As Alya screamed for help, Marinette found the strength she had felt just yesterday and knew what she had to do. She grabbed the black jewellery box and swiftly put the ladybug earrings on, releasing Tikki at the same time.

"I knew you'd come round!" Tikki said, spinning in the air.

"I'm still not sure I can do this," Marinette

said nervously. "But Alya's in danger. I can't just do nothing! Tikki... SPOTS ON!"

As the stone beings marched back to Stoneheart, Ladybug whipped her yo-yo around the car that had trapped Alya. With a swift pull, Alya was released at last. "You can't stay here," Ladybug said, walking past Alya and picking up Cat Noir's baton. "It's too dangerous."

And with that, Ladybug used her yo-yo to catapult herself through the air on the trail of the stone beings.

Before long, she spotted Cat Noir. She tossed his baton to him. "Expand it!" she shouted. Cat Noir used the baton to push open the stone being's hand and free himself from its grasp. Ladybug wrapped her yo-yo around Cat Noir's legs and pulled him to safety. Once again he found himself hanging upside down.

"Lady, have I ever told you, you turn my world upside down?" Cat Noir quipped. He was more than happy to see his partner again, so they could finally teach these stone creatures a lesson. But Ladybug had another plan in mind. She could see the stone beings heading their way.

"You're quite the jokester, but your comic timing could be better." She turned and leapt onto the rooftops, beginning to run away from the beings. "We've got to get out of here."

Cat Noir was confused, but he was starting to realise that Ladybug knew what she was doing. "Aren't we going to take care of them?" he asked, gesturing to Stoneheart's soldiers, who were looking angrier than ever.

"No," Ladybug said as she swung over the rooftops of Paris. "If we want to defeat them all, then we need to get to the heart of the matter... Stoneheart."

CHAPTER FIFTEEN

A Ladybug Promise

Stoneheart roared a primeval cry as he began to climb the Eiffel Tower with Mylène and Chloé in his grasp. The police had surrounded the tower and helicopters circled the supervillain.

On the ground, Chloé's father stood between two police vans, surrounded by armed officers. "I demand my daughter's safe return!" he bellowed through a megaphone.

"Da-deee!" screamed Chloé.

Stoneheart had grown tired of Chloé's

screeching. She wasn't essential to his plan and now he had a way of really teaching her a lesson. "You know what?" Stoneheart barked. "You're welcome to her!" With that, he hurled Chloé off the tower towards her panic-stricken father.

Flying through the air, with only the hard pavement to break her fall, Chloé began to make promises to save her skin. "Help me! I promise I'll be nice to everyone. Say 'please' and 'thank you'..."

Before Chloé could finish her plea, and just moments before she hit the ground, Ladybug swooped in and caught her. She smiled at Chloé, glad she was safe. Despite how she treated people, no one deserved that fate.

"I didn't actually promise to be nice, you know," Chloé scoffed, jumping from Ladybug's arms and running to her father.

It was now time for the police to take action. Lieutenant Roger Raincomprix stood on top of a police van and commanded his officers to attack.

"Wait!" Ladybug and Cat Noir stood in front of the barricade set up by the police. "Don't attack, it will only make things worse!"

Lieutenant Raincomprix looked at Ladybug with disdain. "I have a new plan," he said, waving her away. "Move aside and let the pros do their thing. You've already failed once."

Ladybug's stomach jolted and Marinette's fears and insecurities came bubbling back to the surface. She turned to Cat Noir. "He's right. If I had captured Stoneheart's akuma in the first place none of this would have happened." Ladybug covered her face with her hands. "I knew I wasn't the right person for this job."

Cat Noir had never seen Ladybug like this before. She had always been so confident and in charge. It made his heart ache, especially when he knew how incredible she really was. "No, he's wrong." Cat Noir put a gentle hand on Ladybug's

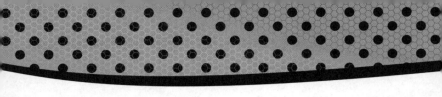

shoulder. "Without you, she'd no longer be here," he gestured towards Chloé, who was being comforted by her father. "And without us, they're not going to make it. We're going to prove it to them. Trust me on this, okay?"

Ladybug stared into Cat Noir's eyes. He had always been the reckless one, storming into battle without thinking. But now Ladybug could see how strong he was, she felt his confidence flowing into her. She smiled back. "Okay."

Suddenly, a strange, guttural coughing distracted the superheroes from each other. They stared at the Eiffel Tower in disbelief. Stoneheart was bent double in pain. What was happening? As he let out one final cough, a giant cloud of black moths emerged from Stoneheart's mouth. Still with Mylène in his clenched hand, his huge stone body fell from the Eiffel Tower towards the ground below.

A terrified crowd watched on as the swarm

of moths took the shape of a colossal face with cruel, pointed features. Then, it spoke.

"People of Paris, listen carefully. I am Hawk Moth."

Ladybug and Cat Noir gasped. "Hawk Moth?" they spoke together, amazed.

Police helicopters circled the face as it continued.

"Ladybug and Cat Noir. If you give me the cat's paw ring and the ladybug earrings, now, all will be well and the stone beings will cease to exist. You've done enough damage to these innocent people."

Suddenly it all became clear. Hawk Moth was the real villain behind Ivan's transformation. Hawk Moth wanted Ladybug and Cat Noir's Miraculouses for his own gain, but Ladybug wasn't about to hand over the precious jewels.

In the silence that followed, only the sound of a slow hand clap could be heard. Cat Noir turned to see Ladybug walking towards the face, unafraid. "Nice try, Hawk Moth," she said with the authority Cat Noir had begun to recognise. "But we all know who the real bad guy is. Let's not reverse the roles. Without you, none of these innocent victims would have been transformed into villains."

Ladybug stood before Hawk Moth's face feeling the strength and power Tikki had promised her would come if she believed in herself. "Hawk Moth, no matter how long it takes, we WILL find you and YOU will give us YOUR Miraculous!" With her threat issued, Ladybug stormed the tower and began to flick and spin her yo-yo at the swarm of moths. "Time to DE-EVILISE!" she cried.

Hawk Moth let out a cry of frustration and anger as the moths crumbled and swirled into Ladybug's yo-yo and vanished. In the moments after Hawk Moth's face had disappeared,

Ladybug turned to the stunned crowd. "Let me make this promise to you," she began, as the television cameras zoomed in and beamed her face across Paris. "No matter who wants to harm you, Ladybug and Cat Noir will do everything in our power to keep you safe."

To emphasise her words she opened her yo-yo, sending a beam of light into the air and releasing a swarm of bright white moths. The crowds surrounding the tower, and the thousands of people watching at home, burst into rapturous cheers of joy. Everyone, that is, apart from Cat Noir who stood silent, rooted to the spot. "Wow," he breathed, impressed.

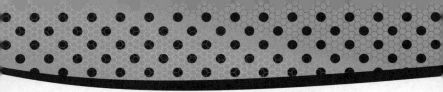

CHAPTER SIXTEEN

It's Miraculous!

Safely hidden in his lair, Hawk Moth was enraged. "That's the trouble with superheroes," he growled. "They're too heroic!"

Hawk Moth wasn't going to be beaten that easily. He still had Stoneheart under his power and he used his force to awaken him. "Stoneheart, they are trying to take Mylène away from you," he taunted. "You must snatch Ladybug and Cat Noir's Miraculouses so they will be powerless against you!"

Lying at the bottom of the Eiffel Tower, Stoneheart's glowing eyes blinked as he received Hawk Moth's message. He lumbered to his feet and Mylène screamed for help once more.

"You'll never take Mylène from me!" Stoneheart wailed, as Cat Noir and Ladybug came together at the foot of the tower. "Come to me, my stone beings!" cried Stoneheart, as he started to climb the tower.

Ladybug and Cat Noir watched as the stone beings clambered up the tower behind him. "What do we do now?" Cat Noir asked. "We're surrounded and we can't attack him with his army of stone soldiers all over the place."

Ladybug had to think of a plan, and she had to think of one fast. "We know where the akuma is," Ladybug said, thinking out loud.

"In his clenched fist, the one he's holding Mylène in," answered Cat Noir.

"And we know he likes Mylène... That's it! We don't need to separate Mylène and Stoneheart, we need to bring them closer together!"

With that, Ladybug swung higher up the tower, leaving Cat Noir clueless. "I'm not really following, but I guess I better trust you. Something tells me this is how it's going to be from now on."

Cat Noir followed Ladybug to the top of the tower, overtaking Stoneheart and Mylène. He landed just as the stone beings began to attack. "How are we supposed to bring them closer than they already are?" Cat Noir shouted. It looked like Stoneheart already had a pretty tight grip on Mylène.

Ladybug grinned. "By using our powers!" Ladybug threw her yo-yo up in the air and cried, "Lucky Charm!" A shower of hearts erupted into the sky and produced a spotted parachute. Ladybug stared at the item, a little unsure.

"What am I supposed to do with this?"

Before Ladybug could think of an answer, Cat Noir was flung through the air by one of the stone beings. He landed on his feet, as cats usually do. "Are you sure you know what you're doing?" he called.

"We'll soon find out," she replied, strapping on the parachute and executing the next part of her plan. "Cat Noir, get ready to catch the akuma!"

Ladybug had a plan to get Mylène and Stoneheart closer together, and she knew just how to do it. She skilfully whipped her yo-yo around the hand Stoneheart was holding Mylène in, and around his neck. Using all the strength she could muster, Ladybug pulled the string of the yo-yo so that Stoneheart's hand was lifted, drawing Mylène near to his face. Soon, they were so close that Mylène's lips brushed against Stoneheart's cheek.

Somewhere deep inside Stoneheart, Ivan's heart was beating. When he felt Mylène's kiss on his cold, hard cheek, it was as though a shock wave coursed through him. He didn't want to be Stoneheart any more.

As Ivan rocked backwards, he dropped Mylène and the crumpled sheet of lyrics the akuma was hiding in. Mylène desperately managed to grab onto one of Ivan's fingers, but the akuma-infected paper ball was sent tumbling to the ground. Cat Noir leapt after it, using his baton like a baseball bat to hit the crumpled ball back up into the air, towards Ladybug. Ladybug opened her yo-yo ready to de-evilise it.

What Ladybug hadn't realised was that once the akuma was released, Ivan would no longer be a giant stone being. As he transformed back into himself, Ivan was no longer big enough or strong enough to hold onto the top of the Eiffel Tower – or Mylène.

Ladybug watched in horror as Mylène and Ivan fell through the air. She glanced at the akuma, which was fluttering away out of reach. She had to make a choice: her friends, or the akuma.

There really wasn't a choice to be made. Ladybug dived off the top of the tower. "Cat Noir, you take care of Ivan!" she called as she focused on saving Mylène.

Cat Noir leapt down the side of the tower. Summoning his Cataclysm power, he dug into the side of the tower to create a metal cradle just large enough for him to reach out and catch Ivan as he fell.

As Ladybug soared towards the ground, she caught Mylène in one arm. With her other arm she shot her yo-yo into the sky, catching the akuma. Finally, Ladybug pulled the strap on the parachute and she and Mylène floated gently to the pavement below.

Once she had checked Mylène was unhurt, Ladybug had one last task to perform. She opened her yo-yo and released a bright white, de-evilised akuma into the air. Then she threw the parachute into the sky. It exploded in waves of beautiful red and black spots that swooped around the stone beings, transforming them back into the ordinary citizens they were before. The spots then swirled around Paris, repairing buildings and mending anything Stoneheart or the stone beings had damaged. Everything was as it had always been.

"Are you seeing what I'm seeing?" asked a dazed Ivan, as Cat Noir helped him limp towards Mylène and Ladybug.

"It's beautiful, and amazing," said Ladybug, overjoyed at what she and Cat Noir had achieved. "It's Miraculous!"

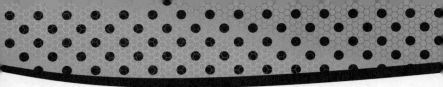

CHAPTER SEVENTEEN

Made For Each Other

*A*s the police cleared away the last of the barricades, Ladybug brought Mylène and Ivan together. "I think you two have a lot to talk about," she said, smiling.

Ivan blushed. He had been too scared to talk to Mylène before, and now after all this, how could he ever tell her how he really felt?

"Maybe it would help if you read the words to Ivan's song." Ladybug handed Mylène the crumpled sheet of lyrics.

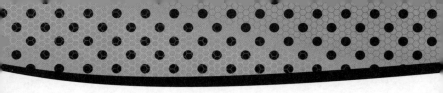

Mylène's eyes scanned the words and she felt her heart lift. "Wow!" she gasped. "It's really beautiful! It's a shame you can't hear the words when you scream, I mean, sing."

Ivan suddenly realised why Mylène had run away when he had performed his song earlier that day. "My singing was scary wasn't it? Is that why you ran away? Because you were afraid of me?" Ivan turned to look at Mylène. "I'm sorry."

Mylène smiled and ran to Ivan, flinging her arms around him. Ivan was so shocked, and so happy, that he froze like one of the stone beings.

"They're made for each other!" giggled Ladybug, as she and Cat Noir watched on.

"Just like you and me," Cat Noir said, charmingly, as he stretched an arm around Ladybug's shoulders.

Ladybug swerved out of his way and caught hold of Cat Noir's wrist playfully, as his ring began to sound its alarm. "Is that the time?

We'd better split. See you soon, Cat Noir."
Ladybug waved goodbye and used her yo-yo
to swing away. They would soon turn back into
their true selves and couldn't risk their identities
being revealed.

"Can't wait, my lady," Cat Noir said with a
smile and a bow.

The following day, Paris was back to normal.
Thanks to Ladybug's powers, it was as though
Stoneheart and the stone beings had never
existed. Alya and Marinette climbed the school
steps, catching up on all the news from the day
before. "By the time I biked to the tower it was
all over," Alya said. She had missed the chance
of an exclusive for her blog.

"Don't worry, you'll get your scoop eventually,"
Marinette said, kindly.

"You're right. Next goal: Ladybug the

exclusive interview! Or better yet, finding out who is behind that mask!"

Marinette giggled. "Good luck with that one," she teased, not noticing the expensive car that had just pulled up behind them. Inside, Adrien was talking to his father via videophone.

"You disobeyed me, Adrien," Gabriel said. "Take a look at that school, it's the last time you will see it—"

Adrien began to protest. His father couldn't take away his only chance at making friends and having a normal life, could he? Not after one day. But Adrien's father hadn't finished. "It's the last time you will see it... without your bodyguards. They will pick you up and drop you off each day. Nathalie will arrange the rest of your schedule for you. You will continue your fencing, Chinese lessons and photoshoots."

Adrien couldn't believe his ears. "Thank you, Nathalie. Thank you, Father!" Without waiting a second longer, he ran out of the car and into school. He couldn't wait to see Nino, Chloé and even Marinette again.

Marinette and Alya walked into class. They were about to sit in the seats they had sat in the day before, but something made Marinette stop. After yesterday she realised she was far stronger than she ever thought she could be. As Ladybug she had superpowers, but as Marinette she had something just as powerful: friendship and confidence. Together, Marinette and Alya sat in the seats Chloé had made them leave on the first day of term. They weren't going to be pushed around any more.

Chloé and Sabrina looked furious as they saw their precious spot behind Adrien was taken. "Er, you're in the wrong seats. Go on, get lost," Chloé demanded.

Marinette smiled sweetly. "All that is necessary for the triumph of evil is for good

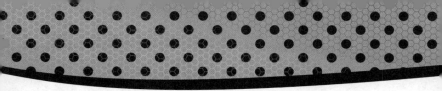

people to do nothing," she said, repeating the words Alya had said to her on the first day they met.

"What is that supposed to mean?" Chloé folded her arms and scowled.

"It means I'm not putting up with you any more, and neither is anyone else, so take your attitude and get lost!"

Chloé was so angry she couldn't think what to say. She didn't even notice Adrien walking into class. Adrien smiled at Marinette, who continued to ignore him. She was still convinced he had something to do with the chewing gum prank Chloé had tried to pull yesterday.

Adrien sat down feeling deflated. He wanted to make the most of school, not have an enemy before he'd even finished a full day.

"Hey, you want friends?" whispered Nino. "Explain what happened to Marinette."

"But what should I say to her?"

"Just be yourself," Nino replied, not realising that being himself was something that had become quite complicated for Adrien over the last few days.

At the end of the day, Adrien still hadn't found the right time to talk to Marinette. As students filed out of school into the pouring rain, Marinette hung back. She might have been more confident, but she was still forgetful and she pictured her umbrella sitting on the kitchen table at home.

Adrien stepped out and opened his umbrella. Now was his chance to make things right. "I just want you to know," he began. "I was trying to take the chewing gum off your seat. I swear."

Something about the way Adrien spoke made Marinette put down her defences a little. She looked at him, willing him to go on. "I've

never been to school before. It's all sort of new to me." Adrien handed his umbrella to Marinette who took it, cautiously.

She looked at the boy that everyone in school was going crazy about and suddenly she understood why. He was a teen supermodel, but as it turned out, he was actually pretty kind, and sort of cool, too.

"See you tomorrow," Adrien waved, skipping down the steps to his waiting car.

"Er, yeah, see you tomo... tom... tomor..." Marinette had lost the ability to form complete words. *Why am I stuttering?* she thought to herself.

As if to answer her question, Tikki flew out of Marinette's jacket. "I think I know the reason!" she teased, giving Marinette a playful hug.

As Adrien reached his car, Plagg jumped out. "One full day at school and you already have an admirer," Plagg laughed.

Adrien shrugged. "Whatever," he smiled. "She's just a friend." Then he gasped. He had a friend at last.

Marinette sighed as she began to walk home under Adrien's umbrella, not noticing the small elderly man who had been watching the two friends from afar.

"Excellent choices, Master," said Wayzz.

Master Fu stroked his beard, pleased with himself. He nodded in agreement. "Those two are made for each other."

The End